# This book belongs to

_____

_____

For my own little cub, Jay, with love
M.M.

First published in Great Britain in 2008 by Gullane Children's Books
This paperback edition published in 2009 by

**Gullane Children's Books**
185 Fleet Street, London, EC4A 2HS
www.gullanebooks.com

3   5   7   9   10   8   6   4   2

Text and Illustrations © Mark Marshall 2008

ISBN: 978-1-86233-757-2

Printed and bound in China

# Little Leopard
## on the Move

By Mark Marshall

GULLANE
CHILDREN'S BOOKS

Little Leopard was happy.
Every day he played with his
friends and snoozed in the shade.
Life couldn't be better.

But one day his mummy had some news.
"Little Leopard," she said, "now you are getting
bigger, we will have to find a home with more space."

"I don't want a new home!" squeaked
Little Leopard. "I like it here,
near all my friends!"

Little Leopard ran off to find Elephant.

"Hello, Little Leopard," smiled
Elephant, "what's with the sad face?"
"Mummy says now I'm getting bigger, we
need a new home," sighed Little Leopard.
"But if we move, I'll miss you!"

"Then why don't you come and live with me?" said Elephant.
"We can splish and splash in the water all day long."

But the water was too cold and wet for
Little Leopard, so he ran off to find the Meerkats.

"Hello, Little Leopard,
what's with the sad face?" asked the Meerkats.
"Mummy says now I'm getting bigger, we need a new home,"
sighed Little Leopard. "But if we move, I'll miss you!"

"Then why don't you come and live with us?"
said the Meerkats. "We can race and dive into
our sandy burrows all day long."

But the burrows were too
small and dark for Little Leopard,
so he scampered off to find Zebra.

"Hello, Little Leopard,
what's with the sad face?" asked Zebra.
"Mummy says now I'm getting bigger, we need a new home,"
sighed Little Leopard. "But if we move, I'll miss you!"

"Then why don't you come and live with me?" cried Zebra.
"We can play hide and seek in the tall grass all day long!"

But the grass was too tickly and scratchy for
Little Leopard, so he ran off to find the Lizards.

"Hello, Little Leopard, what's with the sad face?" asked the Lizards. "Mummy says now I'm getting bigger, we need a new home," sighed Little Leopard. "But if we move, I'll miss you!"

"Then why don't you come and live with us?"
cried the Lizards. "We can sunbathe
on the rocks all day long!"

But the rocks were too hard
and the sun was too hot
for Little Leopard.

Sadly, Little Leopard made his way back to his mummy.

"What's with the sad face, little one?" she asked.

"I don't want to move!" sobbed Little Leopard. "I'll miss my friends."

"Silly thing!" smiled Mummy. "Come with me!"

Little Leopard followed
his mummy through the jungle.
High in the hills was a huge tree with
lots of leaves and branches.
"This is our new home!" said Mummy.

"Wow!" cried
Little Leopard
excitedly, racing
up the tree . . .

"I get my very own branch and
I can still see all my friends!

# Goodnight, everyone!"

# Other Mark Marshall books for you to enjoy

Imagine Me A Pirate!

Little Lion Lost!

Stop, Elephant, Stop!
written by Andrea Shavick

# Other favourites from Gullane Children's Books

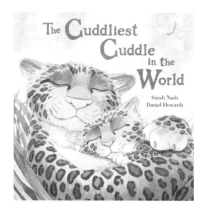

The Cuddliest Cuddle in the World
written by Sarah Nash
illustrated by Daniel Howarth

Penguins
written and illustrated by Liz Pichon

I Love You Always and Forever
written by Jonathan Emmett
illustrated by Daniel Howarth